THE SPACE SPIDER

Peter Bently
Duncan Beedie

On Planet Pok, monsters from all over the galaxy are getting ready for the Monster Olympics. San, Pem Pem, Nid, and Gop join the parade.

Pem Pem enters the race for the Fastest Monster on Planet Pok. On your marks, get set—GO!

Pem Pem zips past all the other monsters to the finish line. Hooray!

Next, Gop wins first place for the Twistiest Monster. She twists so much that it takes forever for San, Nid, and Pem Pem to unravel her.

Nid easily wins the prize for the Strongest Monster.

Then it's San's turn. She can fly really fast, and everyone thinks she's going to win the Fastest Flying Monster race.

San was almost at the finish line when something flashed past her. It was a giant Space Spider. It zoomed across the line to win the race.

Hib jowjow!

San flew back to her nest and sulked.
The other monsters tried to cheer her up.

Pem Pem baked her some
blue broccoli cookies.

Gop juggled some Emerald Rocks.

Then Nid walked upside down on his hands and pulled a funny face.

But San didn't even smile—until Nid sneezed and tumbled into the Sticky Toffee Stream. SPLOP!

San laughed and said sorry for sulking. It was only a race, after all. She invited her friends to stay and share the cookies.

Maig thull chorlap

But first San popped over to the Fizzy Fountain to fetch some lemonade.

On the way, she spotted something in the Glass Bubble Gulch. It was the Space Spider!

San decided to congratulate the Space Spider for winning the race so she flew down to greet it.

San landed next to the spider and said...

Chowl! Zoob blosher bip

...but to her surprise it made a loud buzzing noise and zoomed away.

Boim corb trock?

San tried to follow the spider, but it flew out of sight behind a big rock.

San heard a loud CRASH! She zipped behind the rock and saw the Space Spider lying on the ground. It had flown straight into Nid!

But that wasn't all. The spider wasn't even a real monster. It was a robot. Only real monsters were allowed in the Monster Olympics. Someone had cheated!

San opened the hatch. Inside were two Mudlings! They grinned sheepishly.

Flard loosh!

The Mudlings were very sorry. They had only cheated because Mudlings never won anything. They were too small, too slow, and couldn't fly.

Woylizz stroot!

San had an idea. She would help the Mudlings if they promised not to cheat again...

The monsters went back to the Monster Olympics to collect their medals.

The judges declared San the real winner of the Fastest Flying Monster race.

At the end of the ceremony, the judges announced a special prize. It was for the Best Monster Robot. The winners were the Mudlings!

Moffer sprob thurn!

San invited everyone back to her nest to celebrate with some blue broccoli cookies.

Crub pairsh crubbob

But to her surprise, the Mudlings climbed into their Space Spider and flew off!

Before the monsters could say "pring, prang, bosh" the Mudlings had returned. They had gone to get lemonade from the Fizzy Fountain!

Jallox prith burmell sib

Reading with your monsters!

Monsters' Nonsense is all about having fun while learning the skills of reading. If children have fun reading, they'll want to do it more.

What helps children with their reading?

Phonics: the ability to sound out (decode) words that they don't know.

Reading comprehension: to read for meaning so that they can understand and enjoy the story.

The *Monsters' Nonsense* series is designed to support these skills to help children become successful, happy readers and to encourage a positive, shared reading experience.

The adult reader (or reading mentor) reads the main narrative—supporting reading comprehension and bringing the story alive.

The child reads the Monsters' Nonsense in the speech bubbles. These are "non-words" to help them practice their decoding skills at a level that is right for them. It's important that your child knows that these "non-words" are not real words and have no meaning.

More monster fun

Monster Questions Ask your child questions about the story. For example, who won the prize for the Strongest Monster? What did he say when he won? What did Pem Pem bake for San? What did the Mudlings fetch from the Fizzy Fountain? Who won a special prize? Why? Which event do they think they would be best at in the Monster Olympics?

Magnetic Monsters Ask your child to make some of the non-words in the monsters' language using magnetic or play letters. Make it a real challenge by setting a timer! (An empty biscuit tin is a great place to store magnetic letters and the lid becomes a magnetic surface.)

Mixed up Monsters Choose a real word from the story and then mix up the letters (on paper or using play letters). Then help your child to unjumble the letters to spell out the word. Ask your child to jumble some letters for you to make a word. Use a timer to see who can do it the quickest! For example, somnret – monster, pymliocs – olympics, ccbrooli – broccoli, nonfuita – fountain.

Monster ABC Cut out letters from the alphabet (or use play letters) and place them in order. Try to lay them out in an arc so all the letters are easier to see. Ask your child to point quickly to the first letter of Gop's/San's/Pem Pem's and Nid's names. Repeat for the middle letters and finally the last letters.

Phonics glossary

blend to blend individual sounds together to pronounce a word, e.g. s-n-a-p blended together reads snap.

digraph two letters representing one sound, e.g. sh, ch, th, ph.

grapheme a letter or a group of letters representing one sound, e.g. t, b, sh, ch, igh, ough (as in "though").

High Frequency Words (HFW)
are the words that appear most often in printed materials. They may not be decodable using phonics (or too advanced) but they are useful to learn separately by sight to develop fluency in reading.

phoneme a single identifiable sound, e.g. the letter "t" represents just one sound and the letters "sh" represent just one sound.

segment to split up a word into its individual phonemes in order to spell it, e.g. the word "cat" has three phonemes: /c/, /a/, /t/.

vowel digraph two vowels which, together make one sound, e.g. ai, oo, ow.

Playing with letters is a great way to help children read and write. It's lots of fun too!

Quarto is the authority on a wide range of topics.

Quarto educates, entertains and enriches the lives of our readers—enthusiasts and lovers of hands-on living.

www.quartoknows.com

Publisher: Maxime Boucknooghe
Editorial Director: Victoria Garrard
Art Director: Miranda Snow
Editor: Sophie Hallam
Designer: Mike Henson
Consultant: Carolyn Clarke

First published in the United States in 2016 by QEB Publishing, Inc.
Part of The Quarto Group
6 Orchard
Lake Forest, CA 92630

A CIP record for this book is available from the Library of Congress.

ISBN 978 1 60992 866 7

Printed in China